The Cemetery Dance

Level 5G

Written by Lucy George
Illustrated by Ayesha Lopez Rubio
Reading Consultant: Betty Franchi

About Phonics

Spoken English uses more than 40 speech sounds. Each sound is called a *phoneme*. Some phonemes relate to a single letter (d-o-g) and others to combinations of letters (sh-ar-p). When a phoneme is written down, it is called a *grapheme*. Teaching these sounds, matching them to their written form, and sounding out words for reading is the basis of phonics.

Early phonics instruction gives children the tools to sound out, blend, and say the words without having to rely on memory or guesswork. This instruction gives children the confidence and ability to read unfamiliar words, helping them progress toward independent reading.

About the Consultant

Betty Franchi is an American educator with a Bachelor's Degree in Elementary and Middle Education as well as a Master's Degree in Special Education. Betty holds a National Boards for Professional Teaching Standards certification. Throughout her 24 years as a teacher, she has studied and developed an expertise in Phonetic Awareness and has implemented phonetic strategies, teaching many young children to read, including students with special needs.

Reading tips

This book focuses on the *s* sound
(made with the letters *ce*) as in prin**ce**.

Tricky and/or new words in this book

Any words in bold may have unusual spellings
or are new and have not yet been introduced.

> **Tricky and/or new words in this book**
>
> **know once creatures
> zombies ghouls ghosts
> witches friends**

Extra ways to have fun with this book

After the readers have read the story, ask them
questions about what they have just read.

Who went to the cemetery dance?
*Can you remember three words that contain
the s sound made with the letters ce?*

You'll have the
night of your life! Did I say
night? I meant fright.

A Pronunciation Guide

This grid contains the sounds used in the stories in levels 4, 5, and 6 and a guide on how to say them.

/ă/ as in p**a**t	/ā/ as in p**ay**	/âr/ as in c**are**	/ä/ as in f**a**ther
/b/ as in **b**i**b**	/ch/ as in **ch**ur**ch**	/d/ as in **d**ee**d**/ mill**ed**	/ĕ/ as in p**e**t
/ē/ as in b**ee**	/f/ as in **f**i**f**e/ **ph**ase/ rou**gh**	/g/ as in **g**a**g**	/h/ as in **h**at
/hw/ as in **wh**ich	/ĭ/ as in p**i**t	/ī/ as in p**ie**/ b**y**	/îr/ as in p**ier**
/j/ as in **j**u**dge**	/k/ as in **k**i**ck**/ **c**at/ pi**que**	/l/ as in **l**i**d**/ need**le** (nēd'l)	/m/ as in **m**o**m**
/n/ as in **n**o/ sud**den** (sŭd'n)	/ng/ as in thi**ng**	/ŏ/ as in p**o**t	/ō/ as in t**oe**
/ô/ as in c**augh**t/ p**aw**/ f**or**/ h**o**rrid/ h**oar**se	/oi/ as in n**oi**se	/o͝o/ as in t**oo**k	/ū/ as in c**u**te

/ou/ as in **ou**t	/p/ as in **p**o**p**	/r/ as in **r**oa**r**	/s/ as in **s**au**ce**
/sh/ as in **sh**ip/ di**sh**	/t/ as in **t**igh**t**/ stopp**ed**	/th/ as in **th**in	/th/ as in **th**is
/ŭ/ as in c**u**t	/ûr/ as in **ur**ge/ t**er**m/ f**ir**m/ w**or**d/ h**ear**d	/v/ as in **v**al**ve**	/w/ as in **w**ith
/y/ as in **y**es	/z/ as in **z**ebra/ **x**ylem	/zh/ as in vi**s**ion/ plea**s**ure/ gara**ge**	/ə/ as in **a**bout/ it**e**m/ edibl**e**/ gall**o**p/ circ**u**s
/ər/ as in butt**er**			

Be careful not to add an /uh/ sound to /s/, /t/, /p/, /c/, /h/, /r/, /m/, /d/, /g/, /l/, /f/ and /b/. For example, say /fff/ not /fuh/ and /sss/ not /suh/.

Did you **know** that
once a century,
on Halloween night,

ever since time began,
something happens right
here in this cemetery?

When the moon glances off gravestones, and the wind blows in the trees,

the deceased rise from their graves and **creatures** of the night join them for a dance.

It's the cemetery dance
of the century.

Creatures of the night gather every hundredth Halloween for this party.

Zombies pounce and drink
juice from poisoned chalices.

Ghouls wail with forced, loud voices.

Centaurs prance and
bounce with grace.

Ghosts flounce in their best lace dresses.

Vampires grimace and
act like menaces.

17

Witches embrace and entice old **friends** to join them.

They all dance together.

They dance, prance,
flounce, and bounce.

Do you know what?

They don't cease until the sun comes up. They dance all night long.

When it's all over, they make themselves scarce. They don't leave a trace.

Take my advice, and don't go looking because you might not be able to handle the pace.

OVER **48** TITLES IN SIX LEVELS
Betty Franchi recommends...

Some titles from Level 4

The Circus Mice — 978 1 84898 783 8

Monster's Night — 978 1 84898 784 5

Jemima The Spy — 978 1 84898 785 2

Other titles to enjoy from Level 5

The Gigantic Bear — 978 1 84898 787 6

Celebrity Celia — 978 1 84898 788 3

Goose Flight — 978 1 84898 790 6

Some titles from Level 6

Hugh is New — 978 1 84898 791 3

Clumsy Eagle — 978 1 84898 792 0

Bad Zombie Movie — 978 1 84898 793 7

An Hachette Company
First published in the United States by TickTock, an imprint of Octopus Publishing Group.
www.octopusbooksusa.com

Copyright © Octopus Publishing Group Ltd 2013

Distributed in the US by
Hachette Book Group USA
237 Park Avenue, New York NY 10017, USA

Distributed in Canada by
Canadian Manda Group
165 Dufferin Street, Toronto, Ontario, Canada M6K 3H6

ISBN 978 1 84898 789 0

Printed and bound in China
10 9 8 7 6 5 4 3 2 1